I0624597

LETTERS FROM THE OLIVE TREE

Amazon #1 Bestseller

REESE BALDUCCI

Veridian House

Printed in the United States of America.
Format and design by Veridian House.
Cover design by BCZ.

ISBN - Paperback: 979-8-9988133-1-3
First Edition: April 2025
Current Edition: May 2026

IN TRIBUTE TO

my great-grandparents,
Giovanni (1881-1951) and Ersilia (1888-1973)

*"Give me your tired, your poor, your huddled masses
yearning to breathe free."*
Lazarus, Emma. "The New Colossus."
Statue of Liberty. 1883

"All that I am or ever hope to be, I owe to you."
Abraham Lincoln (paraphrased)

DEDICATION

"A mother's love endures through all."
Washington Irving

To my mother, Linda, unconditional love personified.

I

Pistoia, Tuscany, 1905

THE VERDANT HILLS ABOVE PISTOIA bore their age like a noble crown. They rose in soft terraced folds, green with olive groves and orchard rows that caught the sun in open palms. To the unknowing eye, they appeared merely picturesque, a Tuscan postcard created from a memory. But to the Olivi family, they approached the sacred. These prima hills, so-called as the first foothills of the Apennines, had cradled their bloodline for centuries.

Giovanni Olivi was born into this soil as the second son of a fruit and olive farmer whose lineage ran deeper than the tangled roots of the trees he pruned. Before memory, Giovanni's soul was carved into this land, carried by sun-warmed winds and the muted whispers of twisted vines. He was not from this land. He was of it.

Their farm was humble but enduring. Stone by stone, row by row, it was sculpted by soiled hands and stubborn hearts. Their ancestry acquired the land in the fifteenth century as a gesture of thanks from a local lord for their allegiance during some now-forgotten feud. That grant transformed their family from laborers to landowners, though that line of distinction remained razor-thin. Giovanni's father, Alessandro, often told the story, "Our hands may be calloused, but they are free."

Alessandro rose daily before the sun and silently shouldered the Olivi family legacy without complaint. He never once left the hills of Pistoia. To him, leaving was forgetting, and forgetting was betrayal. The land gave, and they gave back, not in a sentimental exchange, but in covenant. He loved the land and dreamed in its language.

Giovanni absorbed his father's reverence for the land long before he understood it. At first, Giovanni couldn't tell whether his father had forged the land or had been forged by it. But, as the harvests came and went, Giovanni and his older brother, Angelo, grew to appreciate their father's unspoken devotion to the land. They understood his bond not from what he said but from the silence they shared beside him as they walked the orchard rows barefoot, with the brown clay dust clouding around their ankles like breath from the soil itself.

Their mother, Maria, was a woman shaped by time and resilience. She moved between the kitchen and garden as though tethered to both. Her voice was rarely raised but lingered heavily in the house's shadows. She taught Giovanni that when held with care, silence could speak more truth than a thousand well-meant words.

As the years passed, such unspoken lessons came into greater focus for Giovanni and Angelo. The brothers grew into young men, and their lines of inheritance became clear. Angelo, as the eldest, would remain. He would inherit their meager estate. Giovanni, though never addressed directly, would not.

And so a disquiet began to grow in Giovanni, steady as the swirling wind through the hills' valley. He began to wake early and walk alone, not to inspect the trees or count the rows but simply to see what lay beyond the next rise. Sometimes he would bring a book and read beneath the ancient olive tree that marked the corner of their field. Like the tree, with its branches twisted in conversation with the sky, Giovanni pondered: *What else might a man be if not what the land required of him?* In the distance, the bells of Pistoia tolled midday. Their sound floated over the hills, reminding him that time moved on relentlessly even here.

By late autumn, the olive groves thinned into a silvery hush. The golden sun, sitting lower in the fall sky, cast long shadows over the field's edge. Standing apart from the ordered rows, the ancient olive tree stood with its roots gripping the earth, half exposed like old bones. Every conversation that mattered to Giovanni had taken place beneath its shade.

She was already there when he arrived.

Ersilia Innocenti grew up just beyond the ridge on a smaller farm amid neglected trees and rutted fields. The eldest of five, she carried responsibility with unshakable clarity. Her father was sharp-tempered, with a taste for discipline. Her mother, a quieter force, was frayed at the seams by the strain of harvest and household. Ersilia reflected her mother's composure but not her submission. She moved with precision and spoke with economy.

Sitting quietly on the low stone wall, her shawl gathered close, Ersilia braced against more than just the cold. Her chestnut hair was loose at the temples, brushed by the stiff breeze. Her deep brown eyes held a stillness that Giovanni longed to feel in himself.

They had not planned to meet. They rarely did. Yet, somehow, they always found each other here.

"I wasn't sure I'd see you," Ersilia said.

"Neither was I."

It had been this way for years. They grew older, but the distance between them never did. There had been no declarations, no sudden change from neighbors to something more. They had simply happened, natural and certain.

Giovanni stepped toward her, his boots pressing softly into the brittle grass. His exposed cheeks were reddened by the crisp wind.

"They say it will be a dry winter," Ersilia said in time.

Giovanni nodded. "The well is already low."

"My father wants to cut back the fig trees near the barn," she said. "He says they haven't given enough fruit to be worth the water."

Giovanni looked east toward the Innocenti farm as if he could see the struggling trees from afar. "That's a mistake," he said flatly.

"I told him that," she said. "He didn't listen."

Giovanni shifted his weight. "He rarely does."

A crow passed overhead, its cry slicing through the bitter air. They stood silent for a while, stretching the moment.

Ersilia broke their stillness again, her voice low and hesitant. "Do you ever wonder if this is all there is?"

He studied her, unsure whether she meant the land, their duty, or the unspoken closeness neither dared name. Perhaps all of it.

"I wonder," he said finally. "But I don't let myself often."

"Why not?"

He hesitated, cautious of what he might speak into existence. "Because I'm afraid of the answer."

Ersilia nodded, not quite in agreement but in understanding.

"I once thought I would live and die on that farm," she said, raising her eyes to meet his. "Now I'm not sure."

Her words surprised him, though he didn't show it. "Your family needs you, Ersilia."

She sighed. Dropping her head, she stared at her shuffling feet against the stone wall. The wind shifted. The olive tree groaned behind them. "Sometimes I think this old tree knows everything we've ever said."

"Maybe it does," he replied. "It's heard it all."

They shared a gaze but not a smile. Something else, something closer. But still, neither of them spoke of leaving, their words buried somewhere in those silent roots.

When sparse rain finally fell as winter arrived, it barely sprinkled the cracked orchard floor. Leaves browned and fruit withered. The olives, far smaller than they should have been, fell too soon or not at all. Even the once wild and green terrace vines slumped now in exhaustion, the incessant dry days having wrung the will from them.

Giovanni could feel the mounting losses in Alessandro's growing silence, longer now and heavier, like a story he'd forgotten midway through. He watched as his father hunched over the ledger each night, resting his finger between entries that no longer totaled anything useful. Yield was down. Costs were up. The well that once sprang forth with ease had turned sluggish with silt. When Alessandro thought no one was watching, he rubbed his temples as if trying to press back time.

That winter, more than one family from the prima hills sold off a row of trees or a corner plot to settle their accounts. A few disappeared entirely, erasing themselves from the land they had failed to tame. They left before dawn, as quiet as regret, searching for something that might yield.

Giovanni rose one frigid morning to find his mother seated at the kitchen table, her hand resting lightly on an unopened envelope. Her expression was distant, troubled. Drawing nearer, Giovanni saw the smudge of a blue American postmark and, just beneath it, his name written in a familiar scrawl. It was from Michele Gori.

Without a word, Maria held out the envelope. Giovanni sat across from her and read the letter in silence. His eyes moved slowly over each line, pausing occasionally, not to decipher the words but to absorb their weight. When he finished, he folded the page with care and slipped it into the inside pocket of his coat. He said nothing, but Maria, watching him with a mother's knowing eye, saw that something in him had changed.

Michele and Giovanni had grown up together, sharing the same valley. Their days were marked by similar chores and shared mischief. When they weren't helping their parents on their respective family farms, they tossed stones into the same stream, ran through the same market stalls, and spoke in the shorthand of best friends who never needed to explain themselves. Michele had left Pistoia during an earlier lean year, seeking work at the docks in Naples before continuing on to America. His letters came sporadically but loyally, each a small dispatch covering the miles he'd crossed and the life he was building.

Now Michele was in Brooklyn, laying track with a railroad crew that worked the city's outer edges. The noise never settled there, and the air carried the bite of metal and smoke. The days were long, the labor merciless, and the bread tasted faintly of coal. He slept in a narrow tenement room with three other men, their lives stacked like the wooden crates in the street market. But there was money. Michele had saved enough to send a few *lire* back to his mother and buy a new pair of boots before winter.

That night, as he prepared for bed, Giovanni reread the letter.

"It is not a soft life, Giovanni," Michele wrote, "but I know what I'm building every day I work. No one can take it from me."

Giovanni read the letter repeatedly until the words blurred as the candle beside him burned low. At last, he folded the page carefully, almost reverently, and slipped it under the mattress. That night, his dreams were not of departure but of difference. He dreamed of a life he could share with the only soul he couldn't imagine living without.

He rose early, silently working the rows with Angelo. Giovanni told no one about the pull he felt inside him. It was a heavy rope, tight across his chest, tugging him toward something beyond the horizon.

Walking back from the field one evening, he paused beneath the olive tree. The sky had already turned, streaked with the cool lavender of an early dusk. Giovanni rested his hand on the rough bark and pressed his forehead gently to the trunk. The tree had withstood famine and flood, feuds and frost, and the turning of more seasons than any man could name. Still, it offered no guidance in its silence, only the weight of having endured.

The morning lay still like glass, waiting to break.

Rolling fog hung low in the valley, softening the lines of the terraces and transforming the olive trees into hazy silhouettes. Giovanni followed the winding stone path to the corner of the field. His hands and face were cold, but he scarcely noticed.

Beneath their tree stood Ersilia.

Light skimmed across her long braid, setting it aglow with fine strands of copper. She was looking across the valley, toward the slope where her family's land lost itself in stone and bramble. Walking toward her, Giovanni realized he had no clear memory of when she hadn't been part of his world. By the time they were old enough to understand longing, it had already taken root between them.

Giovanni's love for her had no clear beginning. It seemed to have always been. His devotion was quiet and steady, as sure as water slowly carving stone. He loved the calm in her silences, the keen edge of her wit, and the way her eyes seemed to read what he hadn't yet admitted to himself.

He had always known, quietly at first, the limits of what he could offer her here. What began as a whisper had grown into a clamor inside him, loud and insistent, like the town's bells tolling some truth he could no longer ignore.

She turned slightly as he approached, but didn't greet him. She didn't need to.

"I received another letter from Michele," he said, "from America." He paused, giving space for her to react.

A long breath passed through her lips. "He writes often."

"Often enough," Giovanni replied. He watched a slight shift in her shoulders, drawing tighter across her back.

"And what did it say?" Her voice was even and calm.

Giovanni looked toward the far ridge. "He's laying track in Brooklyn. The work is hard. The city seems even worse."

She pressed her lips into a thin line, holding back the words she didn't trust herself to say aloud.

"He sleeps in a flat with three other men," Giovanni continued. "He sends money home. Buys boots when he can."

"That's not a life," she said, finally turning to face him.

"It's a beginning."

He expected her to argue. Instead, she looked at him quietly, steadily, as though weighing something much heavier than what had been spoken.

"Does he sound happy?"

Giovanni hesitated. "No. But he sounds certain."

"I've realized I want more than this," Ersilia said. "I understand now that wanting something different isn't the same as being ungrateful."

He looked at her more closely then. "You want something different?" he asked.

"I want something that's mine," she said.

He stepped closer. The cold cracked between them, but her presence warmed him. "I want that too. I want to wake up knowing the day belongs to me, and I can work for something I can hand down. Something I can build for us."

Ersilia's breath caught at the word. *Us.*

She lowered her gaze, and her voice softened. "You're not afraid?"

"I'm terrified."

She looked back up at him, surprised.

"But that doesn't matter," he said. "Fear can't stop me from dreaming."

She looked away for a long while. Gazing into the valley below, where the fog settled. "I want to believe you," she said.

"Then do."

Giovanni reached for her hand. Their fingers met, and for a moment, neither spoke. He could feel the warmth of her skin even through the chill.

"I'll write," he said. "Every week if I can."

She nodded, but her grip tightened just slightly.

"And when you do," she said, "don't tell me the streets are golden. Don't lie about the work. I don't need comfort. I need the truth."

He nodded. "I will."

He looked at her intently, noticing the rose bloom of cold on her cheeks. "I'll work until there's something real to show for it. I'll send for you. I promise."

She was steady and unsentimental. "How long?"

"As long as it takes," he replied instantly.

She reached into her pocket and pulled out a small length of pale blue ribbon, frayed at one end. "It was my mother's," she said, handing it to him.

Giovanni took it gently. The fabric was soft from age and handling and held a faint lavender scent.

"Keep it," she said. "So you don't forget what you're working for."

"I could never forget," he said solemnly.

She stepped back, measuring her words. "I've always known you would leave," she said. "Long before Michele's letters. Long before the failed harvests. You've had one foot beyond these hills since we were children."

Giovanni remained silent, acknowledging the undeniable truth of her words.

She looked past him. "These hills wait forever," she said softly, with finality. "But I won't."

Then, without another word, she turned and walked away.

He lingered beneath the olive tree, holding the ribbon as a vow, aware that the heartache of distance had just begun.

Standing on platform number two at the train station in Pistoia, beneath a parchment-colored sky, Giovanni bid an emotional farewell to his family and the only home he had ever known. He stood with his single suitcase beside him, his coat buttoned to the throat, and Ersilia's ribbon tucked safely in the inner pocket over his heart.

Angelo clasped his shoulder with a firm but silent understanding. He promised Giovanni that he'd keep their family farm alive despite the mounting hardships. His younger sisters, Elena and Emilia, cried inconsolably. Their tear-streaked faces would be forever imprinted on him as a gut-wrenching memory.

Alessandro stood a few steps apart from the rest of the family, arms crossed and dry-faced. He had said little when Giovanni made his decision and less since. He betrayed little emotion, although Giovanni knew their separation weighed heavily on his soul. They exchanged a short, formal, and silent handshake.

Maria stood close to him, wearing a black dress with a matching veil covering her head. She clutched a rosary in one hand and a linen handkerchief in the other, although she did not cry. Maria was no stranger to such pain and heartache. She was the unshakable rock to whom all others would cling when life's storms assailed. Maria pulled down on Giovanni's broad shoulders, leveling their faces. She tenderly kissed his forehead, mouthing a silent prayer for his safe passage, and handed him the rosary wrapped in the handkerchief. "For the crossing," she whispered.

The train for Genova shuddered into view, lumbering down the tracks toward them. The engine huffed plumes of dark smoke into the bleached morning sky. Giovanni boarded and sat near a window streaked with grime. Leaning his forehead against the cold glass as the train pulled away, he didn't wave. Instead, he watched the figures of his family fade into the landscape. Eventually, even the hills disappeared, swallowed by distance and time.

Genova, Liguria, 1905

The massive iron hull of SS *König Albert* glided into Genova's harbor through water heavy with the sharp scent of brine. The docks swelled with movement as workers shouted in dialect and families clung together in tight knots of fear and hope. Giovanni stood in the crowd waiting to board, his name inked onto the passenger manifest with hundreds of others.

He passed through the boarding checkpoint and descended into the belly of the great ship with the others, guided by the current of movement. His steerage accommodations were dim and crowded. Narrow berths were stacked two and three high in long lines, and the air was stifling. The compartment reeked of too many bodies with too few comforts.

Giovanni claimed a lower bunk between a Sicilian bricklayer and a mother with two coughing children. The space was barely large enough to sit upright, and the mattress was a thin sack of straw, damp with salt and sweat. He stowed his suitcase at his feet and sat with his back against the wall, the ribbon Ersilia had given him tucked now between the pages of a small notebook. He unwrapped his mother's rosary and slipped it over his wrist.

The ship lurched, ropes were cast, and slowly, almost imperceptibly at first, they began to move.

The sea waited ahead, vast and unknowable.

II

The Atlantic Ocean, 1905

CURLED INTO THE NARROW SPACE of his bunk, lonelier than he dared admit, Giovanni wrote to Ersilia by lamplight in words he would carry with him until he reached a place where they could find her.

Ersilia,

The sea seems infinite. It moans and breathes like something living. But I still hear your voice when I close my eyes.

I have the ribbon you gave me nearby. It reminds me of what this journey means. I keep my mother's rosary wrapped around my hand. I am not alone here, though I have never felt so far from home.

There is no sun down here, only the dim glow of oil lamps. So, in this darkness, I remember how you looked beneath the olive tree the last time I saw you.

I know the road ahead will not be easy, but it will lead us together again to a place we can call home.

Wait for me.

Giovanni

Upper New York Bay, 1905

SS *König Albert* steamed into New York Harbor under iron-gray clouds. Giovanni stood near the upper deck rail, his coat pulled tight against the salt wind, and watched as the city emerged through the mist. The ship groaned as it slowly came to port, and Norddeutscher Lloyd Line dock workers moved in quickly, securing ropes to the ship's gigantic iron bollards.

Giovanni clutched his suitcase and stepped into the flow of bodies, descending the narrow wooden gangplank onto the churning platform below. Ellis Island pulsed with motion and noise. Children cried, women murmured prayers, and men shouted names into the din, desperate not to lose each other in the crush. The air was dense with steam and coal smoke, laced with the raw, metallic tang of industry.

The great hall was filled with pioneers like Giovanni; their faces exhibited a blend of emotions: excitement, anxiety, and exhaustion. Although their clothes were filthy, and their spirits were weary, their wills were certainly not broken. Many clung to small bundles tied with cloth or covered in tattered newspapers. Others held fast to their loved ones. Each waited with painstaking anticipation to see whether they would be granted entry to the United States, or, rather, sent back to their native lands, forsaking any chance they might have at a better life.

Giovanni moved with the crowds, waiting for hours, inching toward the inspection booths at the chamber's far end, where men in uniforms waited behind tall desks. The walls of the room felt impossibly high. A barrel ceiling arched overhead, studded with iron beams and glass. Even the windows seemed unreachable.

Ahead, a young woman was pulled from the line after a coughing fit. Her husband shouted and tried to follow, but was held back by a guard. Their child, too young to understand, began to scream.

Giovanni's stomach tightened.

"Next!" The word came sharp and sudden, slicing through his thoughts.

Giovanni stepped forward. His legs were unsteady. The man behind the desk was broad-faced, with a badge pinned to his chest and a pen gripped in one ink-stained hand. "Hello," Giovanni muttered softly and half-heartedly. It was one of only a handful of English words he learned on the boat. He was insecure about trying them out at such a critical moment and instantly regretted saying the word.

"Papers," the inspector said flatly. As he extended his hand forward, his gaze was fixed on Giovanni.

Giovanni could not understand his words, but he had watched enough people before him go through the process and knew how to hand over his travel documents. With trembling hands, he passed them through the small hole in the window without speaking.

The officer scanned them quickly, then looked up for the first time. His eyes were pale and unblinking.

"Where are you going?" he asked.

Giovanni didn't understand. The words pelted him like stones. His mouth opened, but nothing came. The flush of confusion rose hot against his neck. He turned slightly, eyes scanning the room. Faces blurred around him.

In desperation, he met eyes with an older man in the adjoining line. Unlike the hardscrabble Giovanni had traveled with, the stranger was clean and well-dressed. He appeared to be educated and a businessman of some sort. Sensing Giovanni's growing despair, the man warmly spoke to him and said, "*La tua destinazione.*" His voice carried no urgency, only understanding.

Giovanni turned back to the inspector.

"Brooklyn," he said quickly. The word emerged more as a question than an answer.

The inspector grunted, unimpressed. "Where in Brooklyn?"

Giovanni blinked, then reached into his pocket and retrieved a folded slip of paper. He passed it forward. On it was the scrawled name and address of Michele Gori, his friend from Pistoia, his lifeline in America.

The officer copied the information without comment. He flipped through the papers again, tapping his pen once against the edge.

"Can you speak English?" he asked accusatorily.

"A little," Giovanni nervously replied, utilizing another key phrase he had learned while on the ship.

The inspector paused, then leaned forward slightly.

"This isn't Italy," he said coldly. "You work hard, keep quiet, and maybe you'll last."

Giovanni nodded, unsure whether his agreement was required. He didn't understand the full meaning, but he felt its shape.

The inspector lifted a round stamp from his desk, violently pounded it on the page, and handed the papers back to Giovanni.

"Go."

And that was it. No welcome. No ceremony.

Giovanni was ushered through the wide metal gate and into the exterior lobby area of the processing hall. As he exited the immense building alongside other successful immigrants, he noticed the rain had passed, and the sun shone through the clouds.

Ersilia,

I stood before a stranger today who asked me where I belonged, and I said a place I'd never seen.

The men here look tired in their bones. The buildings touch the sky.

I don't fear the work. I welcome it.

I will turn my hands to anything that helps me keep my promise to you.

I have chosen you still.

Giovanni

Brooklyn, New York, 1905

The streets of Red Hook were more raucous than the Atlantic.

When Giovanni stepped off the East River Ferry, he entered a world he could not have imagined, even in his boldest or bleakest thoughts. The city surged. Trolleys screeched against steel rails. Horses clattered past, pulling wagons overloaded with barrels, crates, and the weight of furious commerce. Newsboys shouted headlines he couldn't understand. Even the sky felt crowded, choked by soot from the trailing smoke of chimneys and factories.

Michele found him near the pier, standing awkwardly with his suitcase and papers in hand, gawking at the whirlwind around him. His voice was hoarse with the familiar music of home. "*Dio mio,* Giovanni. You look like you've seen a ghost."

Giovanni turned, and the distance between the prima hills and America vanished momentarily. Michele was leaner than he remembered. The boyish roundness of his face had been traded for the course geometry of survival. But when he smiled, Giovanni saw the same glint of mischief in his eyes that once flashed during the market day in Pistoia.

They embraced without words. Men here didn't linger in affection, but for a heartbeat, Giovanni held to it anyway.

Michele lived in a rental tenement just off Columbia Street near the docks. The stairwell smelled of boiled cabbage, and the dingy wallpaper peeled from the corners. The apartment was barely the size of Giovanni's kitchen back home, consisting of two small rooms with paper-thin walls and even thinner mattresses. There was a communal water tap on the ground floor and outhouses around the back for the residents to share. Giovanni brought the total to five men sharing the space, which was much too small for all to be home at once.

Giovanni was given a mattress near the window. The pane was cracked and let in more wind than light. There was no space for his suitcase, so he stored it beneath a small table by the door. No one cared. Everyone was exhausted.

That night, Michele made chicory coffee and reheated leftover brown lentil soup in a dented tin. They sat on overturned orange crates and tried to talk over the rattle of streetcars below.

"Tomorrow," Michele said, "you will come with me to the rail yard."

Giovanni nodded. He didn't ask about wages or if the job was dangerous. He already knew.

The work was brutal.

They laid track through the outskirts of Brooklyn, past busy warehouses and riverbanks. They slogged through marshland that sucked their boots from their feet. The crew mainly comprised immigrants, including Italians, Irish, and Poles, as well as a few Black men from the South. They were bound together not by choice but by necessity.

The men swung sledgehammers in twelve-hour shifts, driving iron spikes through frozen ground. The air stank of tar and sweat. Splinters worked their way through gloves. Shoulders burned. Skin cracked. Some days, Giovanni's hands bled so severely that he couldn't close them around his fork at night.

Each evening, he returned to the Red Hook flat, his muscles hollowed out and his thoughts quieted by fatigue. He'd rinse with cold water from a basin, bandage his palms, and eat silently beside Michele and the others. Then, often for long hours after the others had drifted asleep, Giovanni would sit alone by the cracked window. He would hold the ribbon Ersilia had given him, its lavender scent now nearly faded, and breathe through his suffocating heartache.

Her first letter came on a Tuesday.

The envelope had been left on his mattress, set there by Michele. Giovanni instantly recognized her handwriting, but he didn't open it immediately. He stared at it for several minutes, his hands shaking and his heart pounding. The instant he opened it, her voice filled the room.

Gio,

Your letter arrived two days ago. I read it standing at the gate before I even came inside. My hands were cold from the morning air, and the ink had bled slightly from the damp, but I understood every word.

I've never seen the ocean, but I imagine it must be beautiful and terrible, impossible to predict. I am glad you crossed it. I am so happy you made it.

I keep picturing you with your hair windblown, squinting toward something distant. I hope your feet are on firm ground now.

Here, I wake up early and work late. In between, I reach for you, like when I pass the olive tree. I expect you to be near. When you are not, I pretend you are just beyond the ridge, reading under our tree.

I've stopped saying your name aloud. It makes everything feel smaller.

I want to ask you everything: What does the sky look like there? What do the streets smell like? Does anything remind you of home? Do you feel changed?

Write soon. Tell me everything.

You left with a purpose. Hold to it.

Ersilia

Giovanni folded the letter slowly, running his fingers over her name. He tucked it back into its envelope, placed it inside his suitcase, and sat still beside the window.

Outside, Brooklyn roared with indifference. But inside him, her voice lingered, crossing the ocean to rest in him like the warmth of another season.

Rural Virginia, Near Richmond, 1906

The news came at midday. It was abrupt and final.

The men had returned from laying track beyond Gowanus Creek, their shirts soaked in tar and rain, their boots caked in mud and industrial ash. They were gathering their personal things at the day's end when the foreman stepped up, read a short notice from the railroad company, and announced that funding for their rail section had been cut.

No wages would be issued beyond the day. No work would follow.

Just like that, Giovanni's time in Brooklyn was over.

Michele found a job unloading freight at the Red Hook terminal, but there were no openings for Giovanni. Another friend from Naples mentioned work farther south. Rail lines were being constructed through the wetlands and pine forests beyond Richmond. It wasn't guaranteed, but it was something to keep hope alive.

Before daylight the next morning, Giovanni packed his things in silence. He wrapped Ersilia's letter in an oilcloth and placed it carefully beneath his coat in his suitcase. He embraced Michele in gratitude and then closed the door behind him. Both men knew they would likely never see one another again.

After dropping a letter for Ersilia into the train station's Cutler mailbox chute, Giovanni boarded a southbound train. He didn't know the route and didn't ask about the schedule. He sat by the window and watched the city unfold as he drifted further away. Eventually, the dotted skyline surrendered to long sweeps of trees and Virginia's low, red clay hills.

The labor camp outside Richmond was nothing more than a row of canvas tents pitched along the edge of a half-cleared forest. The railroad company had struck a temporary deal with the local landowners, gaining access in exchange for progress for the locals.

Progress, however, meant bodies. And in this part of the world, bodies were cheap.

Giovanni was paid in cash, and his meals were beans and salt pork ladled from blackened iron pots. The men slept on beds of pine needles and moss, covered only by ragged wool blankets. Giovanni rolled his dirty clothes into a ball, creating a makeshift pillow. The night sounds were not of crickets or owls but men groaning in muted desperation.

He worked beside Aldo Martinelli, who was also from Tuscany and had once been a shoemaker's apprentice in Lucca. Aldo had a gentle spirit and a kind heart. He carefully bandaged Giovanni's split knuckles after a hammer slipped and struck his hand. In return, Giovanni shared his ration of bread.

On the sixteenth day of work in a row, Aldo collapsed mid-swing beside Giovanni.

The foreman ordered the others to keep working as Giovanni knelt beside Aldo.

But Aldo did not stir. By nightfall, it was clear he would not. Fever gripped him. His eyes rolled back in his head. When he stopped breathing, only Giovanni cared.

Giovanni dug the grave in silence behind the tents. He found an old sack to wrap around Aldo's body and silently laid him in the earth. That night, Giovanni could not sleep. He sat by the fire long after it had gone to embers, Ersilia's ribbon in his hand. The sweet scent was gone now, and all that remained was its feel, rough and threadbare.

He wrote to her the next day.

The letter was short and cautious. Giovanni didn't say how many men had left the camp, how many were sick, or how little money he had left. He mailed it from a post office in a one-road town.

Then he waited.

And waited.

He returned to the camp each night and asked the man who handled deliveries if a letter had come.

Nothing.

Weeks passed. The silence widened.

He wrote again. This time, the words came differently. Not guarded, but urgent. Not hopeful, but restless. But this time, he tucked the letter into the lining of his suitcase instead of mailing it, unsure whether he could allow the words he had written to be given life outside of his head.

Ersilia,

If you have forgotten me, I understand. I do not say that to hurt you. I say it because I know the world changes, and sometimes people change, too.

I have nothing to offer you right now but this back-breaking work. Each day, I swing a hammer into this black ground that swallows everything. There is no rest. The sky here is too dark. The nights are too long. But still, I see your face when I close my eyes. It is the only thing that comes to me without fail.

I am still trying to build something for us, although most days it feels like just a dream.

But whatever it becomes, it is yours. Even if I never get to give it to you.

Giovanni

Giovanni never showed the letter to anyone. But when the loneliness pressed hardest, he would unfold it, hold it in his lap, and reread it.

Her ribbon stayed with him, too, though the color had faded to something closer to ash.

He did not know whether Ersilia was still waiting or had moved on to another.

Either way, he only knew that if her love for him still lived, it might run like a silent rail hidden in miles of darkness until one day, when it surfaced again in the light.

And so, he swung the hammer.

And still, he hoped.

Mississippi Delta, 1906

Giovanni left Virginia as most men did that season, without a destination. The railway section was completed, and agricultural work, like the fields themselves, had dried up. Word of wages further south drifted through the camp, unreliable but enough to keep the men moving.

Without the money to buy a passenger train ticket, Giovanni hopped a freight car headed south. He didn't know where it would stop until the wheels slowed alongside a stretch of Delta farmland soaked in humidity and desolation. Mississippi wasn't a decision. It was literally the end of the line.

He arrived with only his suitcase and a slip of paper bearing the name of a man he had left in the unforgiving ground. The last of his coins had been spent on bread. With no other option, he followed a cold trail of rumors to a small cotton plantation just outside Shelby, where a landowner who needed strong backs asked few questions.

It was sharecropping by name but servitude in practice.

Giovanni shared a shanty with five other men, its roof sagging under age and rain, its floor simply dirt and mud. In trade for his labor, he received seed, tools, and credit that ran a deeper red than the blazing Delta sun. By the time Spring's first shoots broke through the thick gumbo soil, Giovanni owed more than he could repay.

Still, he planted. He chopped. He bowed his back for belief.

Then came the rain. At first, the fields welcomed it. Bolls opened to drink in the lifeblood of growth. But when the rain refused to relent, the ground turned into impenetrable mud, as black as coffee grounds and just as bitter. Cotton rows stretched as far as sight drowned where they stood.

Giovanni stepped into the waterlogged rows, the black earth grabbing at his steps. In the center of the field, he fell to his knees and gently cradled a crushed root in his hands. His breath was ragged in his throat. The sky above him was a restless, distant, and mournful grey.

There, among the mire and ruin, Giovanni wept bitterly. Not the muffled tears of exhaustion but full-bodied, sorrowful despair. He wept for the seed he had sewn in the ground and the faith he'd buried with it. He sobbed for every hour bent beneath the torturous sun, for the hunger he had swallowed like pride and for the silence that had widened between him and the woman he still wished to call his. He had come to this place with only a clenched fist and a vow he intended to transform into a home. But the land had swallowed him whole, and the sky casually spat him out. At that moment, Giovanni felt the crushing weight of his loss. It was the tireless, steady erosion of a dream too long unmet. Sharecropping didn't steal a man's will all at once. Instead, it unraveled him, season by season, until even the soil forgot his name.

And worse still, he feared that Ersilia, far and fading, might already be gone from the future he hoped to build.

Giovanni did not write for weeks. There was nothing to say. When he finally did, his words bore the scars of his rejection.

He continued about his days in silence, waking before dawn to barter at the plantation's commissary or muck the ditches that filled with fresh silt after each new rain. At night, he sat on the shanty's porch and stared into the flat horizon, searching for anything that might look like a future.

Giovanni had tucked away Ersilia's ribbon in a worn bag at the foot of his bed. He couldn't bear to look at it. The once rich and colorful symbol of their commitment was now a dark and brittle reminder of his collapse.

Then, a letter.

It had been forwarded twice and carried by hand for the last hundred miles. It was worn at the corners and stained. He sat down on the porch steps and opened it slowly, afraid of what it might contain and perhaps more fearful of what it wouldn't.

Gio,

I have written you twice since receiving your last letter from Mississippi, yet I have received nothing in return. I do not say this to accuse you. I know there must be reasons. I tell you only so you will understand the silence I've felt.

I worry for you, Gio. Your letter sounded as if you were losing hope. Do not. Hold on to our dream. I pray for you. I pray for us.

Every few weeks, my father asks what I plan to do. He does not speak your name. He speaks only of time, seasons passing, and what girls owe to the homes that raised them. He reminds me that the land is not forgiving. I remind him that neither am I.

But I do grow tired. Not of you. Never of you. Only of the waiting.

And yet, I have not said yes. Not to anyone. I hope this letter finds you. I hope your heart is not too far from mine. Write soon, if you can. I miss you.

Ersilia

Giovanni folded it with trembling hands and pressed it to his chest. No tears came. Only the slow unwinding of a heart held tightly clenched for too long.

That night, he sat in the doorway with the ribbon beside him and Ersilia's letter in his lap.

The floodwaters had receded.

She had not said yes.

Once again, hope lived.

III

Shelby, Mississippi, 1906

THE HEAT MERCIFULLY SOFTENED BY September, but the land remembered summer's cruelty. The fields were pale, half-starved, half-recovering, like a sick animal learning to stand again.

Giovanni was mucking the drainage ditch near the farm's commissary when he heard two of the overseers talking. One mentioned that some of the plantation's land was being sold off, part of the old estate now being divested by inheritance. Giovanni stood up straighter and listened.

"After Boss Alexander passed this summer," the man said, spitting tobacco into the dust, "a niece of his from up north inherited the entire plantation." He wiped his face with a dirty bandana he drew from his back pocket. "Far as I hear, she's looking to be rid of this whole place."

The other man grunted. "Can't say I blame her. This farm is rotted clean through. That bottomland is so overgrown from flooding that it ain't worth the back taxes it's racked up."

Giovanni was already walking.

A clerk at the courthouse in town directed him to a boarding house where the niece was staying. It was a two-story antebellum that had barely survived the war, only to suffer what appeared to be a slow death from derelict and disrepair. Giovanni bound up the wrap-around wooden porch's front steps and knocked soundly on the glass pane of the front door.

The landlady answered the door with a look of mixed confusion and annoyance. She ushered Giovanni inside to the sitting room. The space was spare and still, with curtains drawn to soften the light. A frayed lace runner sat atop a sideboard, and on the mantle, a clock ticked loudly in the hush. It smelled of cotton gin dust and wool cloth. Giovanni felt the room was meant for waiting, not for living.

Clara Alexander arrived in short order.

She was younger than Giovanni expected, no older than himself, really. Her dress was plain but tailored, and her soft blonde hair was tightly pinned. She spoke in the clipped rhythm of a Northerner that Giovanni recognized from his time in New York.

"May I help you?" she offered.

"I am here about the land," Giovanni replied, removing his hat. He nervously brushed out the folds of his dingy work pants and breathed deeply. "I heard you might be selling some of it."

"What's your name?" she inquired.

"Giovanni Olivi," he stated. It was the first time he had said his full name out loud since he arrived at Ellis Island.

"Where are you from?"

"Tuscany," he said with as much of his heart as his mouth.

"Do you work on the farm?" she asked.

"Yes, this is my second season."

She studied him. "You're a sharecropper?"

"They call us field hands," Giovanni replied. His shame had burned off long ago, along with the notion that survival required apology.

Clara motioned him to sit near the open window in one of the straight-backed wooden chairs, and she sat across from him in the other. Her expression softened slightly. "I inherited the entire property after my mother died," she said with a hint of regret. "My uncle died without a will. He was a beast of a man, with no wife and no children," she said contemptuously.

Giovanni shifted in his chair, the urge to speak rising like a boiling pot. But his mother's old counsel echoed in the back of his mind, restraining him to exercise silence as wisdom in moments like these. He swallowed what he wanted to say about her uncle, the memory of that man's cruelty still too close to trust with words.

She continued. "Everything passed to my mother, his sister and only heir. But she passed away almost a year ago. They had been estranged for quite some time." Clara said with a wistful tilt of her head. "So, I ended up with everything."

"Then… will you be keeping the land?" Giovanni asked, trying to steady his voice. A burst of self-doubt bolted through him. Had he misunderstood what he'd overheard? Had his limited English turned a whisper of hope into something never truly offered? He felt a knot tightening in his throat, and his stomach turned over.

She gave a short, humorless laugh. "Not a chance. I am from Chicago. My mother was a maid for a hotel near the train depot. I have a job as a secretary for a professor at the university. I belong to the city, not to *this*." She gestured vaguely, waving her hand above her head. "Whatever *this* is."

Giovanni nodded with relief, unsure whether she was bragging or apologizing.

Clara stiffened her back and raised her chin. "I am here only to settle the estate. I'll sell the portion of the land that is ready now, and then I will work on selling the rest later, the part that needs to be cut and cleared."

She paused in reflection for a moment before she continued. "I don't have the money, or the stomach for that matter, to manage '*field hands.*' And I have no patience for bondage disguised as agriculture."

Giovanni took notice. "Sharecropping?"

She nodded, her voice sharpening. "It's legalized theft. I've seen the ledgers. Men are paid fractions of what they're due, all while owing more at the end of a season than they did at the start. It's a vicious circle of deception and dependence."

"Desperate men have to survive." Giovanni tread lightly. "Sometimes it's the only way."

She leaned forward, her voice low but steady. "I'll be honest with you. I don't want to be here, but I also don't want to see this land continue to be a tool that evil men keep using to enslave others. I want it to go to someone who will break that cycle."

Giovanni glanced toward the window. The wooden porch rail was warped and splintering; the paint had long worn away. "I don't have much money," he said. "I haven't been able to save very much."

Clara nodded in unspoken understanding.

Giovanni pressed forward. "I do have something else of value, though."

"What else do you have?" she asked.

"My hands and my back," he answered. "I can give them to you as I have given them to this land."

Clara considered him for a long beat, balancing her decision between economics and humanity. She stood and walked over to a corner table covered with papers, retrieving a survey map the attorney had prepared for the estate. "I have an idea," she said, spreading the map onto the spindled Victorian-style coffee table in front of them.

Giovanni edged forward in his chair, studying the map as though it might reveal a way out, not just from poverty but from the anguish that had settled over his life.

Clara gestured. "Do you see this parcel outlined here in red?"

"I know that field," Giovanni said, focusing on the map. "They called it the pecan field. It was flooded out, and the cotton was destroyed. They abandoned it after the flood, and now it has become overgrown."

"That's right," Clara agreed. "Also, once they abandoned it, my uncle quit paying its property taxes."

Giovanni had no notion of what land taxes cost. It was the kind of detail that never trickled down to men like him who worked the soil but never owned it.

She turned the map ninety degrees on the table to redirect their attention. "Now, see this parcel?"

"Yes," Giovanni said, "That field borders the bayou."

"Correct." Clara pointed to the blue line on the map, indicating the stream that fed the bayou. "My uncle never cleared that land, never farmed it."

"That's right." Giovanni nodded in agreement.

She turned toward Giovanni, rising from the map. "But the survey shows that most of that field is above the flood plane. If it were cleared, it would make a suitable field for farming. It would be worth a lot more money."

Giovanni watched her closely, beginning to sense where the conversation was headed. He sat forward, his voice firm but quiet. "I can clear that land," he said. "I've cleared worse."

Clara gave the faintest nod, the corners of her mouth lifting in something between a smile and a concession. "Then I think we can make a deal."

She turned her eyes back to the map, gathering her thoughts. Across from her, Giovanni fought to steady his breath. A piece of land to call his own was no longer just a dream, whispered in exhaustion. The reality began taking shape before him, created in lines, ink, and possibility.

Clara returned to her chair with an envelope she had taken from the table. Giovanni nervously followed to his chair, anxious to hear her next words. "Giovanni, I'll sell you the pecan field for what's owed on its taxes." She handed him the envelope. "This is the tax bill."

Giovanni opened the envelope with trembling hands and scanned the invoice, reading the total due at the bottom of the page. It was more money than he had currently, but it was achievable with a few more months' savings.

Before he could respond, Clara continued. "But you have to do something for me."

Giovanni exhaled sharply. "What else?"

"I want you to clear the bayou field. I'll give you until next planting season to get it done. That way, you can work your land at the same time you are clearing mine." Clara folded her hands in her lap. "I can get three times the value for that field after it's cleared."

Giovanni lowered the envelope slowly, allowing the moment to settle into his bones. "This... " he began, then stopped, searching for the words. "This is more than a sale. It's a chance I feel like I've been waiting a lifetime for."

He drew a breath, steadying his voice. "I promised someone a long time ago. I told her I would make a life that I could ask her to join. Before now, I've had nothing to offer her except a dream." His eyes met Clara's, earnest and raw. "But this? This is something I can put in the ground and watch grow. Something that can be ours."

That afternoon, Giovanni signed the promissory note and deed in the clerk's office. At dusk, he walked every row of his newly purchased field until the sun touched the tip of the west end row. The land was wildly overgrown with kudzu and honeysuckle and silted with alluvial sand from the nearby river. A lone pecan tree stood in the northwest corner, marking the survey boundary.

Giovanni sat on the ground beneath the canopy of the proud, old tree and took the ribbon from his pocket. He drew his knees to his chest and unfolded a piece of paper.

As the crickets started to chirp, he began writing the most important letter of his life.

Ersilia,

I have done what I promised.

There is land now. Not much, but enough. Enough to build something together that will last.

I will begin clearing the rows in the morning. I will turn the soil every day with your name on my lips.

There is a place here for you. I will build a home for us. Tell your father you are no longer waiting.

Come.

Giovanni

The weeks passed slowly. Giovanni worked the land with a renewed purpose. Each row cleared was a line of silent prayer. He spent mornings in the field and evenings working on the humble two-room cabin he and Ersilia would call home. He tried not to mark the days but noticed their passing just the same, in the softening of the ground, in the return of birdsong, and in the way the light lingered longer on the edge of evening.

She arrived in early spring when the air still carried a chill, but the fields had begun to turn green again.

Giovanni stood alone on the platform, his hands clasped behind his back. The steam locomotive hissed to a stop. He scanned the faces that stepped down one by one.

Then she appeared.

She wore a dark cotton dress with a traveling coat pinned closed at the neck. Her hair was up, tucked into a tight bun. She carried a leather satchel. Her face was thinner than he remembered, possibly from weariness, but her eyes were the same.

She crossed the platform and stood before him. "I thought I would cry," she said softly.

Giovanni took the bag from her shoulder, setting it gently on the ground. "But you didn't."

"No," she said. "I'm too relieved."

They didn't embrace right away. Instead, they stood as they were. Then Ersilia reached for his hand, and he took hers.

The cabin was still rough, but she said nothing of the cracks in the floorboards or the way the wind slipped through the door's seams. Instead, she stood in the center of the room, her hands on her hips. "It smells like beans and dust," she said, smiling through a quiet laugh.

That evening, they ate bread and jam on the porch. Ersilia spread a cloth across their laps and poured water from the well bucket into two tin cups. The porch creaked as they leaned against the railing, their shoulders brushing. They talked about her voyage over the Atlantic, the train ride, the weather, the goats back in Pistoia, and how they never listened to anyone who told them to give up on their dream.

The sky turned violet, and the first stars broke through. "This land is good," she said.

He looked across it, the field now in shadows. "But it's not what makes this home."

She turned to him. "What does?"

He reached for her hand. "You do."

That night, they lay down side by side in their small bed, the window open to the sound of grasshoppers and cicadas. Giovanni listened to Ersilia's breathing as it slowed. The ribbon she had given him now lay threadbare but still whole on the windowsill.

He no longer needed to write. She was here now. The life he had promised her had begun.

The wait was over.

About the Author

Reese Balducci is a fiction writer who explores themes of perseverance, longing, and the quiet heroism of everyday life. A lifelong admirer of rich, character-driven storytelling, he draws inspiration from his family's deep Italian roots and is passionate about history, particularly the immigrant experience in America.

As a dual citizen, Reese lives in the American South and Tuscany, surrounded by the landscapes and histories that continue to shape his work.

www.reesebalducci.com

LETTERS FROM THE OLIVE TREE

Acknowledgements

I am deeply grateful to my wife, Amy, for her unwavering support and encouragement.

I am also thankful to the wonderful people of Pistoia, Italy, who have welcomed us with open arms and hearts. Their kindness and generosity have changed our lives.

Although fictional, this story is based upon my great-grandparents' real-life experiences as immigrants to the United States from the Comune of Ostra, Province of Ancona, Region of Le Marche, Italy, near the turn of the century. Their hardships portrayed herein were authentic, as were their indomitable spirits and enduring love. I owe them everything.

www.ingramcontent.com/pod-product-compliance
Lightning Source LLC
Chambersburg PA
CBHW050916120626
46552CB00004B/1595